Narrations in a Nutshell

*An anthology of original short stories, poems,
word-play and essays*

Mr. Charles F. Pletcher

ISBN: 099078651X
ISBN 13: 9780990786511

Forward

I'm a bottom line kind of author. If you're a busy person who takes pleasure from the escape a good story can provide but can't find the time, you'll appreciate the brevity of each work in this book.

All twenty-four are quick reads.

I can't think of any story ever written that could not be condensed to fifteen pages or less. Some communication experts maintain a single paragraph might even be enough. Why, then, do we have to endure the other three hundred pages of embellishment?

I have a friend who told me she liked my short stories because she could start and finish each one over her morning coffee, an evening cocktail or a luxurious bath.

As a businessman, I listened to my customers. As I writer, I listen to my readers. Thus this anthology: three compelling short stories; fourteen entertaining shorter stories, an essay and a few silly poems thrown in to add a touch of humor.

All original, three have won awards. The rest are unpublished, though they've all been read and enjoyed by my friends. I hope you enjoy them as well.

Charles F. Pletcher

THIS BOOK IS DEDICATED TO PAT VERMETTE

PART V---SHORT & PERSONAL

PART VI---SILLY POEMS

PART I
SHORT STORIES

I

Brotherly Love

When Sally's husband divorced her, the pain was so devastating she sought professional assistance. In an effort to avoid an imminent substance abuse problem, her therapist suggested she try a different approach. He taught her the art of visualization. Every day since then, Sally imagined her heart being secured with a thick coat of sealing wax before even getting out of bed. At first this helped contain the hurt, which was crippling her. But over time, it became a defensive technique to ward off all potential suitors, providing her the emotional freedom she needed to focus on her two young children and her job.

For three years, this is how Sally started her mornings---until yesterday. Yesterday, she forgot to lock the door to her heart.

Was this omission simply an oversight or a subconscious attempt to finally test the perilous waters of a new social life? Neither explanation crossed her mind as her workday began at the Alan Stern, CPA firm, where most of the clients were like those you'd find on your favorite TV show; that is, if you like to watch "America's Most Wanted".

Spotting the striking young man at her desk as she finished setting up the coffee, Sally did a double take---thinking he was Richard Gere. She soon realized he was too young.

Smiling as he glanced at her name plate, he said, "Good morning Ms. Adkins. I'm Joey Licatta, Sal's son. Mr. Stern is expecting me at ten but my plane got in early."

"Let me call and see how close he is," she replied, "Traffic coming into Miami this time of day is wicked. Can I offer you some coffee?"

"With cream, please," he answered, taking a seat.

"Alan's only minutes away," she said, handing him a hot steaming cup of her boss's special grind, "but I'm so sorry to hear of your father's death, he was my favorite client, always asking about my kids and often bringing in presents for them and sometimes for me as well."

"That didn't bother your husband by any chance, did it?"

"I'm not married!" she answered, with an awkward croak.

"Oh, that's right, now I remember," Joey lied, "In fact, my father spoke of you often."

"He did?"

"Yes, and he told me if I ever came into town to be sure and ask you to dinner."

"I'm sorry but we have a rule here about socializing with the clients."

"But, I'm not a client, my father was. I'm only in town this week to settle his estate."

Maybe the sealing wax really had been applied that morning and maybe it was the blushing redness of her cheeks that melted it. Anyway, it must have vanished because she surprised herself by saying, "How would your wife react if I agreed?"

"I have no wife," he replied as Alan Stern entered the office. Joey wasn't lying about that.

Sally had met and married her former husband when she was only seventeen, thinking she was in love. But after sharing dinner with Joey Licatta that night she realized the overpowering emotions, enkindled by his mere presence, were much more profound than she'd ever felt. Throughout the evening her head was bounding with thoughts of Joey ripping off her clothes and the relentless lovemaking that would ensue, regardless of where it might occur---the more bizarre the better. Maybe later on the beach, maybe even in the elevator on the way down from dinner. It didn't matter and she couldn't wait.

The principle reason for Sally's divorce had been her sexual reticence, so this was not at all like her.

These stirrings intensified as he bade her good night with little more than an innocuous kiss. What a gorgeous smile he had. It did things to her in places she'd forgotten existed. And since her ex-husband would have their kids for two more days, she invited Joey over for dinner the next evening. That's when he flashed his final smile of the day. It kept her awake all night.

Sally knew her parents would be thrilled to hear about this young surgeon from Chicago and his interest in their daughter. This would be the answer to their prayers. So she called her mom first thing the next morning, rattling off every detail of her new romantic experience. The enthusiasm and relief her mother felt was apparent throughout their conversation until Sally mentioned Joey's name. Then the dialogue went cold.

"What's wrong, mom?" she asked, "I know about Mr. Lacatta's bad reputation before he retired down here, but to me he was always the dearest, sweetest old man you could imagine. And Joey is so gentle and caring and interesting and...and...gorgeous besides!"

"I'll call you right back," her mother said.

Minutes later her phone rang. "Where can your father and I meet you for lunch? Preferably some place private."

To insure that privacy, her parents, Ted and Verna Mathers, arrived early. Asking the waitress to keep an eye out for their daughter, Verna said, "She'll be easy to spot. She looks just like Audrey Hepburn, but with a better figure."

A few minutes of small talk followed after placing their orders. Then a dead silence occurred. Finally, Mrs. Mathers took a deep breath and put her arms around Sally. "We promised your aunt Tilly on her death bed we'd never tell you what you're about to hear, my sweet child," she whispered.

Taking his daughter's hand and pressing it to his tear stained cheek, her father said, "We're not your real parents, baby."

"What!" Sally screamed, overcome by disbelief morphing into anger. "I've finally found something worthwhile in life besides my kids and my work, and you pick this moment to lay such a bombshell on me. How could you..."

"Hold on Kitten," her father interrupted as Sally yanked her hand back from under his, "There's a reason, a damn good reason because..."

"I don't want to hear it, dad! Not now, maybe never. I've got to get back to work!"

"...your aunt Tilly is your real mother," Ted continued.

This brought Sally back into her seat just as lunch was being served. Pushing it away, she put her head down on her folded arms and began to cry.

Caressing his daughter's head and shoulder, her father looked at his wife, saying, "Maybe you should tell her the rest, dear."

Verna gently lifted Sally's head, saying, "Honey, remember how surprised you were when you got that call from Mr. Stern about a job in his office?"

"Yes, I do remember," Sally sobbed, "He said a friend of mine recommended me but I never found out who that...Why are you asking me this now, Mom?"

"That friend was Salvatore Licatta, himself. Your aunt Tilly was his mistress and... and...he is your real..."

"Don't' tell me! Don't tell me. Don't tell me..."

Almost lifeless now, Sally barely whimpered as her mother continued, "Your first name is actually a combination of both of theirs. We were always afraid you might figure that out on your own one day. But, dearest daughter, you do know what this means, don't you? It means Joey Licatta is...well, your half-brother."

"We are so sorry. We love you and would never do anything to hurt you," her father said. "This is killin' us baby, believe me, but there is no other choice. You have to know!"

The parental issue aside, all Sally could think about at this moment was how disgraceful it was to be possessed by such overpowering lust for one's own brother. She felt indelibly tarnished.

Trouble was, she still longed for him!

Disturbed by the extent of their daughter's anguish, Ted and Verna insisted Sally not return to work. She would go home with them now and her father would leave later that evening to meet Joey at her place.

———

The first thing Joey noticed about the unexpected stranger answering the door was his commanding presence, which towered a good six inches above him. "Must have the wrong address," he blurted, knowing full well he hadn't.

"Not if you're looking for Sally Adkins," Ted shot back.

"I am! Is she here?"

"I'm her father, young man...Mr. Lacatta, is it?"

"Yes sir," Joey replied, extending his hand.

Not returning the gesture, Ted declared, "She asked me to give you her apologies, but she won't be seeing you tonight or any other..."

"Wait a minute. Wait a minute. Is she home? May I talk to her?"

"No and no, Sally's with her mother at our house. She's ill and we don't expect her to return to work for several..."

"I'm a doctor; if she's sick perhaps I can help. Does she know about this conversation or is this all your own idea? Something's not right here!"

They were holding each other's gaze for what seemed like several light-years, when Ted finally offered his hand. "I'm Ted Mathers, Mr. Lacatta. It's been a pretty rough day around here. Sorry to be taking this all out on you. If nothing else, you do deserve an explanation. Won't you come in?"

Five minutes into their discussion, however, Ted became uncomfortable with Joey's total lack of response. "You seem to be enjoying all this, young man, and I don't mind telling you I'm offended!"

"If I appear unphased, Mr. Mathers, it's simply because I'm so relieved to hear what you're saying."

"Relieved? Are you out of your mind? If you care at all for Sally, how could you possibly not realize what this has done to her? Even if your own value system would permit such an unthinkable travesty, Sally finds it deplorable and so do we! And, that's all that matters here."

"May I ask, sir: will there be a time in this conversation when I may be permitted to speak? You might see things differently if you'll simply allow me to respond."

———

Two hours later both men showed up together at the Mathers' home---all smiles. When she saw this, Sally went ballistic. In the throes of a primal shriek, she raced into the bedroom; her mother not far behind. After calming her daughter somewhat, Verna returned to the living room and confronted her husband and Joey, demanding an explanation.

"Let the young man speak, please!" Ted insisted, "You'll see, everything's going to be just fine, dear."

"I never knew my father had a child out of wedlock, but I'm not surprised, though there is no mention of this in his will---at least not in what I've seen so far," Joey told her. "But you see, Mrs. Mathers, it doesn't matter. It's like I explained to your husband: your daughter and I have something very unusual in common. You're not her real parents and Sal and his wife are not mine. They adopted me after my father was killed in the war.

Because my real father was Sal's best friend, it was common knowl-
edge, so I've known this for quite a while but yesterday, Mr. Stern
showed me all the legal papers associated with it for the first time. It
was pretty sobering."

As Joey's message sank in, Verna began to cry, hugging him as he
finished his story, "This is difficult for me to discuss because my mom
was so crushed by dad's death she committed suicide a week after I was
born. The Lacatta's are the only parents I've ever known and more wonderful people I could never wish for. And by the way---and this is the
important thing---I'm crazy about your daughter and I'm devastated at
the thought of her being in such mortal pain. May I see her now?"

"Please make yourself comfortable, son, for just a couple of minutes
while my husband and I have a few words with our Sally. Then I'm sure
the two of you will want to be alone."

"That won't be necessary mom," her daughter announced, peeking
around the hallway corner. "I heard every word he said and I think the
two of us are ready to be alone right now. Maybe you and dad could go
take in a movie."

Despite her red eyes and disheveled appearance, Joey couldn't
remember ever seeing a more beautiful sight as he rushed into her waiting embrace, ushering her back over to the couch, where an emotional
concert of joy and relief played itself out among the four of them.

For certain, the door to Sally's heart had been relocked at lunch that
day---tighter than ever---but it was permanently opened hours later,
welcoming in the man who would soon become her new husband: Joey
Licatta.

II

Adam Won

An attractive coed had just taken a seat at Adam's table. "Hi, I'm Diane," she said, interrupting his lunch, "I got a question for you."

Closing his Botany book, Adam looked up, "Shoot!" he replied.

"We have a bet going on about you and…"

"Which *we* are you referring to?"

"That crew over there by the window."

Adam had noticed a number of 'regulars' frequenting that part of the grill at Bailey Community College and he knew they were definitely cool. He also knew he wasn't. Beyond that, Adam had paid minimal attention.

"Okay, I'll bite, Diane. What's the bet about?"

"I think you went to Catholic school. The others disagree."

Washing down the last vestiges of his lunch, he answered, "You won the bet, Dianne. Congratulations! Now I need to get over to the library and finish my studies before heading home."

After telling her his name, she surprised him, "There's an air about you that gives you away; call it professional, I guess. You know, it's the way you dress and all. That briefcase, too; even your pipe."

Adam got her drift; though, he couldn't recall anyone ever associating a pipe with parochial education. He was strictly no-nonsense when it came to his studies. And the way he dressed helped him stay focused. He'd worn a tie since first grade and still preferred to. As for the cuffed and pleated khakis, button-down shirts and penny loafers; well, they were there out of economic necessity. Paying his own way since tenth grade, Adam simply couldn't afford new clothes or even cigarettes. Pipes were a much cheaper smoke.

"And here I thought it was the permanent ruler-marks on my knuckles that gave me away," he said as they parted.

"You're clever too, aren't you, Adam? I never would have guessed..."

Every day, following his last class, Adam shot over to the grill and started his homework while scarfing down a late lunch. By four, he'd be in the library. It stayed open weeknights until nine and Adam needed every minute. He almost never studied at home; far too many distractions there. And his job at a local diner allowed him little time to hit the books over the weekend, especially if he had a date.

———

"Still studying?" Diane said, breaking his concentration, "I'm impressed."

"Oh, hi! Yeah, the librarian has to throw me out most every night."

They spoke in muffled tones.

"Listen, everybody wants to meet you. So, the next time you're in the grill, stop by my table and..."

"Diane, please! This place closes in twenty minutes. Can we possibly talk about that another time?"

"Just forget it!" she said, raising her voice and stomping off.

When he left that evening, she was waiting outside the library door. "You did say another time, didn't you, Adam?"

In the moonlight Diane looked even more beautiful than he'd earlier observed; a head-turner to be sure---every inch of her. "You know, I'm glad you're here," he chuckled, "I was gonna look you up tomorrow and apologize."

"Apology accepted! So, does that mean you'll be stopping by our table tomorrow?"

"Probably, at my usual time: around 3:30. That work for you?"

"Perfect."

Adam knew he was out of her league and probably that of her friends, as well. Where could she possibly be going with all this?

———

He had to admit they were a friendly group. So much so, it was difficult to break away and get to his studies the next afternoon. Indeed, these people were preppy. It was obvious he wasn't. But they appeared to admire him for that. Their cordial conversation made Adam feel good about himself---not at all what he'd expected.

"Look, this is gonna sound strange," Diane was saying following him to his favorite table, "But, now that you've met the group, could I ask your opinion about a personal problem I'm having?"

"I don't want you to get ticked at me again, Diane, but could this possibly wait til later?"

"How about tonight when you leave the library?"

"Sure."

"Or maybe you could even use some company while you're studying?"

"Look, I don't mean to be rude; but not really. I'm here for an education, Diane, and I'm serious about it, so..."

"I'll be waiting outside the door, okay."

"Well, uh...I guess so."

"How do like your coffee, Adam? I'll bring a couple cups."

"Black is fine."

"I should have known!"

—————

They were sitting in her '63 Karmann Ghia, the hot coffee giving Adam a much needed lift. "You know, this car still smells new, Diane."

"It's not even a year old. It was my graduation gift last June."

"Mine was this briefcase. My parents gave it to me," he said, "Monogram and all. Neither of them finished high school, so they had no way of knowing how out-of-place it would be here in college. But, it serves as a reminder that they want me to make something of myself. I don't intend to disappoint them. I carry it proudly."

"Good for you, Adam. I couldn't imagine you without it."

Was she mocking him? He began to think so.

"Anyway," she continued, "I need some advice about this problem I have, and..."

"What's the reason you're asking me, Diane? I don't get it."

"I need a man's point of view; that's all; and, well...you are a man."

"Looks to me like you have no shortage in that regard. There was a bunch at your table today---every day, as a matter of fact; from what I can see."

"Yeah, but you're a lot different than most of them. More level headed, maybe."

Adam just didn't understand preppy people and he was feeling uncomfortable. Maybe this whole thing was really part of a much bigger bet than he'd been lead to believe yesterday...a bet designed to poke fun at him and his labor-class upbringing, perhaps.

From afar, he'd deemed her clique to be immature, if not brainless. Up close they appeared to be much different. But, was it all part of a gigantic joke? Probably so; they were far too complimentary---especially Diane. Especially right now...

"Anyway, there's this guy," she was saying, "He was at our table today when you met everybody. I can't get him to notice me. I'm dying to go out with him. Maybe he thinks like you just said: that I'm too popular or something. Not really sure. That's why I thought you might be able to help, you see..."

"Forgive my confusion, Diane, but you don't know me from..."

"From Adam?"

"Okay, forget that part. But, I'm a perfect stranger? Why not ask somebody who's close to him? Hey, wait a minute! I just realized you put cream in this coffee."

"I've been waiting for you to say something..."

"You know it's really not that bad...you know what, I like it. I'll be a son of a..."

"Getting back to your question, Adam: if I told the people who know this guy, they'd probably turn right around and clue him in. I'd be embarrassed. You can understand that, can't you?"

Her answers seemed too pat, if not rehearsed. In spite of that, he was falling helplessly under her spell.

"But if he was at your table today, Diane, then I must know him too, right?"

"Okay..."

"So, I might tell him myself, right? You see, anyway you want to look at this, I think you're talking to the wrong person."

"No I'm not! Here's the difference: you don't know who he is and I have no intention of telling you!"

"Diane, can't you see how really childish this is..."

"Should I just be bold and ask him out or use a go-between or I don't know what...It's keeping me up at night. Do you have any opinion about go-betweens?"

"Not really, Diane. Why? Is that what you're driving at? You looking for a go-between, are you?"

"No, not really. I was just wondering; that's all."

Even at his young age, Adam realized the futility of trying to understand women. So, ignoring his own suspicions, he jumped in with both feet. And, for the record, he actually did know why, at least for the moment: it was because she was gorgeous!

"Okay, Diane, let me think about it. I'll pay another visit to your group tomorrow. Maybe I can spot something. But, I'm really lost here... Hold on, hold on! It just hit me. How does this fellow take his coffee? Something along that line might just get his attention. If he truly is ignoring you, offer him a cup and serve it differently; just like you did to me...could start the ball rolling."

"That's what I mean about you, Adam. Your idea is brilliant. Let's see what happens."

She couldn't actually have meant that, he felt; because it was probably the most idiotic suggestion he'd ever made. Adam's uncertainty returned.

———

Other than that stupid coffee scheme, Adam had no other thoughts except for his mounting suspicions. Though, when he stopped by

Diane's table the next day, he had noticed one guy who seemed to be keeping his distance from her.

"Then we'll talk again tonight, okay Adam?" she said as he left for the library.

"Sure Diane, around nine in the parking lot works for me," he answered somewhat taken aback, "Any particular reason?"

"Oh yes! I think your strategy is taking hold but I'll know for sure by the time we meet," she said with a wink.

"Glad I could help," he answered, more sure now than ever he was the brunt of some Machiavellian scheme. She'd never be dumb enough to try that moronic coffee stunt on anybody else, but he didn't care. Adam also sensed this caper was about to end. What concerned him the most was why he didn't want it to...

Beyond her good looks, Diane had a spunky personality. It had gotten to him and it wouldn't let go. Good judgment aside, he began searching for a way to prolong the discourse. This was a side of himself he'd never before witnessed.

———

"I have a surprise for you," she said as they sat in her car that evening.

Saddened, Adam was sure this meant she'd landed her prey. He stiffened his upper lip. "You mean you've put something else in my coffee? Listen, Diane, I don't adjust very well to sudden change."

"You know, you're quite a comic, Adam; aren't you?"

He ignored her question. Instead, sensing the guillotine was ready to fall, he swallowed hard and asked, "About your surprise, what is it? Did you finally get through to this guy?"

"Almost Adam; almost."

"That's the surprise? You almost got..."

"No, no, that's not the surprise. It's something else. You see, all the girls at my table really think you're cute---one, in particular. She's got the hots for you. Loves that Cherry Blend tobacco you smoke. Oh, and she wants to know if the cologne you're wearing is Canoe. I have to confess, she's the reason I approached you in the first place..."

"I thought you had a bet about me."

"We did. I didn't make that up. But it gave me a legitimate reason to approach you."

Now he got the picture. That's why she asked about the go-between. That had to be what this was really all about: Diane was acting as a match-maker for one of her friends. And, as for the mystery man she'd talked about; why, he was probably non-existent.

Just there to hold me in place till I took the bait, Adam conjectured.

Choosing not to play those cards just yet, he said, "I suppose you're going to keep me in the dark about her too, right?"

"Not for long."

"Game over, Diane! I want no part of this!" he heard himself saying, though he wasn't sure why. Later, Adam would realize it was all about the anger and distress he felt knowing their brief trysts were coming to an end. He was trying to protect himself from the inevitable pain certain to descend upon him very soon.

"Game, Adam? What game? Games are something you try to win by making someone else lose..."

"Your point?"

"Okay, maybe this does seem a little *cloak and dagger*, but I'm not trying to win anything that would cause you to lose something. You've got to understand that."

"I've had it with this, Diane. I don't know if you're being straight with me or not. When I look at your friends; you know, the way you guys act, the way you guys dress, well...I just can't imagine that someone in your bracket is interested in a labor class schmuck like me?"

"Where is all this coming from, Adam? I'm beginning to think you feel this is some kind of mockery or..."

"C'mon, Diane! Cut the crap. I could care less about conforming with or impressing any of your type of people...get it?"

"Are you through, sir?"

"For now, yes and in more ways than one," he answered, opening the car door.

Grabbing his arm, she said, "Please, I can't understand why you feel this way. That girl really does exist and right now she's not feeling very good about herself."

"Why is that?"

"She wishes I'd never approached you on her behalf. That's why."

"Okay, so maybe I might believe you, maybe...But why go to all this trouble: making up stories about some fictitious fellow you---of all people---were afraid to confront?"

He'd played his full hand, now. It was all there, laid out on the table. But she wasn't flinching. Diane was sticking to her story.

"Listen, I've been honest with you every step of the way. He really does exist. And, for your information, I know guys who would kill to get a date with that girl who's interested in you."

"You're kidding..."

"Not in the slightest..."

Now Adam was feeling embarrassed. His insecurities were show-ing and, up until that very moment, he'd never realized they existed. Why wasn't he able to simply take Diane at face value? Maybe she was really being straight with him. Maybe it was exactly as she stated: she'd broken the ice with him on behalf of her girlfriend.

But, that wasn't the problem. The problem was he now realized how much he enjoyed---really enjoyed---being with Diane, not her girl-friend. It pained him to know she was about to step aside and into the arms of someone he'd helped her get to.

"She's not hard up for attention, believe me." Diane was saying," In fact, she gets hit on a lot. Even a few of her girlfriends' fathers have made passes."

Recalling there had been a cute girl at that table today who'd smiled at him a lot, he said: "I just want to get this right, Diane. You made contact with me for one of your girl friends. That was the only reason?"

"Correct."

"But then something about me made you want to confide your frustrations about some guy you're carrying a torch for."

"That's pretty close, Adam."

"And your friend, why is she interested in me, anyway?"

"I know she's asked herself that question several times. Anyway, she's been dying to meet you for quite a while. I made it possible. I swear to you Adam, that is the truth. It's that simple; no games, no pranks... nothing else. And, like you just said, after I met you, you struck me as someone...well, you know...who could...I guess that was a big mistake, right?"

"I don't know whether it was or not. But you didn't answer my question, why is your friend interested in me?"

"Who knows? Maybe it's because you have what my dad calls command of presence. You do have that, Adam. You have it in spades!"

"She told you that, did she?"

"She didn't have to."

"Look, I don't know what to think. Why this guessing game here? Something doesn't add up."

"I'm not a liar, Adam. I'm sorry you seem to think so."

"And I suppose you want me to believe you really did pull that coffee stunt on him..."

"I do, indeed."

"When, today?"

"No, Adam, last night."

"You saw him last night?"

"I did."

"But I thought you couldn't...Did you run into him after we...

"Listen, you were at our table today, right? Think about it. He was there. You said you might spot something, remember?"

"I do remember. Actually, I thought it might be that jock, Niles; the one with the letter sweater on. He never once looked your way. And that blond girl sitting next to you; the one with the big hazel eyes, she seemed to show some interest in me. I didn't really think about that until this conversa...Anyway, is she the one...is she?"

Diane showed no sign of responding, so he barked, "Answer me! This guessing game has got to stop!"

"I agree, I agree. Let's end it right now. Niles is not the guy and Sharon, who was next to me, is not the girl. But you're close on both counts."

"What do you mean, close? Close to what?"

"Well first, close to Niles. It's the guy who was standing next to him. Do you recall who that was?"

"No. In fact, I think everybody was sitting. Yes, I'm sure of that."

"Not everyone, Adam."

"You're wrong about that, Diane. I was the only one standing. I'm positive."

"Aha!" She said with a smile as big as Nebraska.

"...you mean...I'm the guy you've been...

Still grinning, eyes wide as saucers, she shook her head.

"...then what about that girl?"

"It's me, silly. She's me. I'm the girl," she whispered.

She was holding his gaze, moisture forming in her eyes. Relaxing her grasp from his arms she caressed his hand. Now, both his hands...

"I'm stuck on you Adam. My foot's caught in your door and I can't get it out. God help me, I think I love you!" She was denied further comment because his lips were in the way...

Diane had been wrong about one thing: it really was a game and it did have a loser and a winner. She was the loser; she lost her heart. Adam was the winner; he won her!

III

Cross *World* Puzzles

B ill James was struggling with the answer to *64 down*. Since retiring last year, he started each day with a hot cup of coffee and a crossword puzzle. This helped him forge the ever-widening gap between sleep and reality. Now he was in the middle of puzzle number 125 from a book of 300, the clue being *The FBI child*. Remembering the daughter of Ephrem Zimbalist, Jr. who starred in The FBI TV series, Bill finally got it. He penciled in *Stephanie*.

This made sense but it gave him serious pause. *Stephanie* was the last name of a girl he'd briefly dated in college almost a half-century ago. Her first name was Laura and she'd been on his mind for quite some time. Recently his longings for her had become compulsive.

Quite a coincidence finding her name in this puzzle, he thought.

Bill couldn't be sure when this preoccupation with Laura had started; or even what caused it. For decades, he'd never given her a thought. Now, this matter had begun to frighten him. Bill knew it wasn't normal. After all, he was a married man and, on the surface, the relationship appeared sound. But last year it showed signs of unraveling. This year, a free fall seemed imminent.

Were his marital problems, in any way, related to this obsession with Laura Stephanie? Bill really didn't think so.

He'd actually dreamt about her the night before. That didn't register until he entered his answer to number *64 down*. By further coincidence, their brief romance had taken place in '64 but that didn't register either...at least not for the moment.

They'd met in the winter semester of his junior year. JFK was dead, Johnson was President and the impact of the Beatles revolution was making its presence felt. She worked in the campus bookshop and had caught his attention on several occasions. The day he made his move, she wore a sweatshirt with *I Want to Hold Your Hand* printed on the back.

"I'm no good at reading minds," he'd said as she turned around, "But I do have a talent for reading backs."

Laura laughed, offering no resistance as he clasped her hand in both of his. The attraction was mutual and instant.

Later that evening, they went for a walk. The snow was chilling, the air was crisp but the warmth, emanating from their young hearts, shielded them from the cold. Snuggling before a majestic fire at the campus skating rink, they shared a steaming cup of cocoa. Smatterings of whipped cream on their lips added to the enchantment of the evening as they shared playful kisses. An hour after saying goodnight to Laura, Bill phoned the girl he'd dated since high school and broke up with her.

That was in February. But by May, Bill and Laura were also history. Try, as he might, he could not remember why, though he knew for certain it was his idea not hers.

Following graduation in 1965, Bill had joined the Air Force, opting for a twenty-year hitch after OCS training. Meanwhile, he met and married his first wife, with whom he had two sons. Five years prior to his discharge, she was killed in an auto accident.

Both boys were currently lifers in the Air Force---just like their dad. His youngest son, Heath, played hockey on the airbase and his team had just won the championship. Their victory photograph would be forthcoming by mail. "Might take a few weeks though, Dad," his son had cautioned. A special spot in Bill's den already awaited its arrival.

He'd married his second wife twenty-two years ago. She was in Knoxville with her Church group the day he worked on puzzle number 125. Sitting on the deck of a mountain condo they'd rented for the week-end, thoughts of Laura Stephanie consumed him.

Until that time, he'd made only cursory attempts to find her. That morning---August 5th, 2011---his search began in earnest. Bill's last answer for the day was *19 across*, the clue being *A man for all seasons*. He wrote down *Al Roker*, the Today Show weatherman.

Putting his booklet aside, he showered and poured another cup of coffee. Wondering what he might say to her if they ever met again, Bill opened his computer and typed in *Laura Stephanie...*

For weeks, thereafter, other coincidental clues and answers began to randomly occur in his puzzles. One sought the shape of a swimming pool, *kidney* being the answer. A can of kidney beans had fallen from an open cupboard onto Bill's foot, just that morning. Then, there was the day he noticed an inordinate amount of irritation in his left eye. The first clue that morning was *Late night flight*; he answered *Red eye*! And so the conundrum continued---incessantly. Before long there were eight such instances.

Convinced someone or something was trying to get his attention and keep it, Bill made a startling discovery. He noticed each case was followed by a relevant and timely occurrence---except for the puzzle where *Stephanie* was the answer. Nothing unusual happened that day; other than the futile search he'd begun.

Thoughts of her embrace lingered on, but he recalled little else. There was almost no ammunition to work with here. She came from a small rural town in Illinois or was it Indiana. No, maybe Iowa. It had a strange name; one or two syllables at most. Could have been Ida---who knows? After weeks of Googling every imaginable combination, Bill was about ready to give up.

Then he remembered her middle name was Jean. For some reason, he hadn't used it in his search. And then there was that local sorority she had joined. So, he started all over. An hour later, he found her picture on a College Year Book web site. Taken in the fall of 1963, Laura Jean Stephanie stood third from the left in the bottom row of Nu Sigma Phi's annual photo. Bill became ecstatic, thinking this might lead to a breakthrough!

Sadly, an exploration of subsequent yearbooks found no further mention of her. Maybe Laura hadn't finished college; at least not there. The real problem was her current last name. She must have gotten married; but when and to whom? Needing another plan of attack, he reexamined puzzle number 125, though not really sure why.

It's theme, *maiden names*, took him aback. He hadn't recalled that. Maybe he was getting somewhere. But then again, maybe not. And why in heaven's name had he become so entangled with this silly pursuit of a distant memory? A sketchy one, at best. Had he lost his mind? This was not at all rational behavior!

Something else occurred to him: hadn't he worked with some guy, a number of years back, whose cousin belonged to Nu Sigma Phi? Yes, yes! He'd even met her at some company function. She had to be at least twenty years younger than Laura but it was worth a try. What was that fellow's name, anyway?

It took a few days to track his buddy down and another week before his cousin, Lily, made contact. "I'm sure I can help, Mr. James," she said, "We have a very active alumnae association. But first, would you mind if I asked the nature of your inquiry? This seems a bit unusual."

"I know we're going back almost fifty years but I've come to realize I left something very precious with her. I wonder if she even knows that."

"What could that possibly be after all this time, Mr. James?"

"My heart, young lady. My heart."

"Wow! Well, my uncle speaks highly of you; and, I think we've even met, haven't we?"

"Years ago, Lily, at our company picnic, I believe. You were wearing a Nu Sig t-shirt and I commented about it and..."

"Yes, that's just where my uncle said it was. And I do remember; you'd just gotten out of the service. He says I told him you were cute or something. Not sure I recall that part. Anyway, I'll do a mass e-mail this evening and be back in touch real soon. But you realize the best I can do, if I even find her, is to let her know you're trying to reach her. I hope you understand."

"I do, of course. I am deeply grateful for your help."

When Bill got Lily's voice mail several days later, he was so nervous he misdialed twice before reaching her. "I'm afraid I have disappointing news," she said, "Of the thirty-five responses I've gotten back, nobody's heard from her since the summer of '64. But I'll keep trying."

In the meantime, Bill and his wife had begun serious discussions about their future together. In fact, she admitted to having located an attorney, with whom she'd met several times.

Another week passed. Bill was now working on puzzle number 136 and its title, *Breaking Up,* had gotten his attention. He saw no apparent pattern, but felt certain all of these crossword peculiarities were related, noting that prior to August 5th, there had been no such incident—not one.

Who in the hell is trying to reach me, he thought while showering. When he finished, there was a text from Lily on his cell, requesting a call. "I think we've got a breakthrough, here Mr. James," she said, "I got an e-mail last night from someone who stayed in touch with Laura well into the eighties."

"Lily, don't keep me in suspense, please! What else have you learned?"

"She got married in 1969 in Bern, Indiana. Does the name of that city ring a bell?"

"I'm not sure, but maybe. Anything more?"

"The last time the two were in contact, Laura was living near Chicago and teaching kindergarten. Married still with three children; a boy and two girls."

"And her name, Lily? I mean her last name..."

"It's spelled R-o-c-h-e-r. I'm not sure how it's pronounced, but I'll find out at lunch today."

"Send me the check for that meal. It's the least I can do. I am so... well...let's just say, I'm astounded."

Bill was choking on those words and needed to compose himself, his first appointment with a divorce attorney being less than an hour away.

"I should be free by two this afternoon, Lily, will you please call me."

"Of course, Mr. James. But, I have to get going. It's a long drive. Keep your fingers crossed!" she said hanging up.

The lawyer Bill selected was Brenda Whitehurst, recommended by both his CPA and his doctor. While waiting in the lobby, he spotted her undergraduate diploma from 1968 and did a double take. They'd each attended the same university.

"You look very familiar," his new attorney remarked as he entered her office, "Have we met before?"

"Until a few minutes ago, I would have said no. But now, I'm not so sure."

"You mean we might know each other?"

"By a strange coincidence, ma'am, it appears we went to the same college; and, we were there together for at least one year."

"You mean State?"

"Yes, ma'am, class of 1965."

"Call me Brenda, please. Do you remember anybody from Nu Sigma Phi, Mr. James? I was its President my last year there?"

"Come again?" Bill could not believe what he'd just heard.

"Nu Sigma Phi, you know the local sorority, I was...."

"Laura Stephanie, I knew Laura well..."

"I just found out this morning about her death," Linda said, "We grew up in the same neighborhood and..."

"Her death; she's dead? When, when did this happen?"

"Just recently I think. I haven't heard Laura's name in years, but somebody from Nu Sig's Alumnae Association's been trying to locate her. I got several e-mails over the last few weeks. I've been so busy I didn't answer. Then late this morning I was copied on another e-mail... Hold on, let me see if I can pull it up. My, this is quite a coincidence, wouldn't you say, Mr. James?"

Bill was white and overcome with chills penetrating to the depths of his being. "I've been trying to reach..."

"Here it is right here, Mr. James. And the obituary's attached. Hold on, we can read it together. Oh, and here's her picture too."

"I'm sorry Brenda, but would you mind just giving me a copy. I'd rather read it in private. You see she and I..."

"You look ill Mr. James. I apologize. I had no idea. I mean this appears to have really affected you. Were the two of you close or..."

"Look, I'll be happy to pay your fee for this meeting, but I have to cut it short. Perhaps next week..."

"Of course, of course...there's no charge. I'm a bit...well, she was my neighbor and I always looked up to her. Made me promise to pledge her sorority when I got to college and all..."

Maybe Bill was dreaming; he couldn't be sure; but he was already out of earshot as Brenda finished her thought. Before leaving, he neatly folded the two printed pages given him by her secretary.

His cell phone vibrated as he approached his car. It was Lily, "I decided to call early because I've got such great news..."

"By any chance, did you check your e-mails after we talked this morning," Bill asked, interrupting her.

"Why, no I..."

"She's dead, Lily," he said, ending the call.

Bill James sat in his car, nervously shuffling the obituary papers. The strain of missing sleep over his impending divorce, compounded by the intensity of his sorrow, was more than he could take. Bill could no longer hold back his tears...

———

Composed now and driving, he called Lily to apologize.

"I just read about it," she said. "The e mail came in right after I left for lunch. So I missed it. How much do you know?"

"I have the death notice with me, Lily, but I want to get home before looking at it. I found out about this by a most bizarre coincidence. You wouldn't believe..."

"Can I tell you some good news?" she interrupted.

"Of course you can if there is any, but I don't see..."

"The lady I met at lunch knew Laura very well and when I gave her your name, she really lit up. Laura had spoken to her often about you,

Mr. James. Quite often! I think there's a big surprise here that you may not be ready for at this moment."

"Go on."

"She was married in '69, right? Oh and, by the way, her last name is pronounced just like Al Roker's."

Chills again overcame him...

"But get this," Lily continued, "Her son was born in January of 1965; January 25th, to be exact; four years before her marriage."

Bill quickly did the math; the last time they were together in that way had been the previous April. It also startled him that the birth date and the puzzle number were both 125. "Do you know his name, Lily?"

"William James Rocher and I was just reading about him in her obituary. He's an officer in the military. With that name, sir; well let me ask you straight out, could he, by any possibility, be..."

"Be mine?" Bill asked, "Did your lady friend comment on that?"

"She said he was, for sure. Heard it directly from Laura herself!"

Of course, Bill was dreaming. This could not be happening, or so he thought...

Somehow he'd gotten home. Sitting in his den, attempting for the third time that day to compose himself, Bill opened the crumpled papers and discovered Laura J. Rocher, nee Stephanie, died that August 5th, the very day he'd found her maiden name in the crossword puzzle.

It must be Laura, He thought, *it had to be.* That's when it hit him: *64 down. That was also the year they'd courted. And Al Roker....Let me see.* He pulled out his booklet, removing the puzzle in question. Sure enough Al Roker was 19 across.

19 across, 64 down; 1964. Now it all makes sense. He wondered about the seven other coincidental puzzle answers over the last two months. Was she simply trying to keep his attention? *That had to be it!*

There were two photos. One quite recent; the other from her youth--- just the way he remembered her. How he would cherish that picture. The very sight of it stirred feelings within him he'd long forgotten. As for the recent photo, she hadn't changed nearly as much as Bill had imagined.

Reading further, he discovered she'd been widowed for ten years prior to her passing, still living in the Chicago area. Both her daughters were teachers---just like their mom. Laura had five grandchildren, the eldest being William James Rocher II. Bill noted the boy should have been called *Junior.* Was this a conscious decision on somebody's part? Could Laura have had something to do with this?

Or perhaps her son---whoa! Wait a minute, our son---wanted to send a signal to the world that this young lad was third in succession rather than second. Bill wondered.

Realizing Laura's love transcended life itself, he pondered what else might lie ahead. And, following his second glass of wine, a tinge of excitement got hold of him. Bill was coming to grips with the magnitude of this miraculous event. He coupled the puzzle with her death-notice papers, pressing them to his chest in warm embrace. Reclining in his lounger, eyes shut, Bill sensed Laura Stephanie's presence and reveled in it for a second or maybe an hour---he would never be sure.

A sudden knock on the door by his wife startled him, dissipating the apparition. Tossing Bill's mail on the floor of his den, she left for the evening. In a desperate sweat, he tried to reconvene his communion with Laura. It could not be restored---not that night nor ever again; though he had no way of knowing this at the moment.

Depressed and frustrated, Bill rose from his chair, stepping on a piece of mail from the pile on the floor. Recognizing it as the manila envelope he'd been expecting from Heath, he quickly came back to reality; that is until he opened it...

It contained the hockey team picture he'd been promised: Heath and several other players, and---oh yes---the coach, holding the Victory Trophy. His name: Lieutenant Colonel William James Rocher, United States Air Force!

PART II
SHORTER STORIES

IV

A Change for the Worse

W hy didn't someone stop me before I entered the Lady's Room at Jethro's Pickle Barrel Restaurant by mistake? The waiting area for seating had been exceptionally crowded. Fighting my way through it, I hadn't noticed the restrooms were positioned opposite from all the other locations I'd frequented.

My name is Lenny Edwards. My boss and I were returning from a charity parade when we decided to have lunch before going back to work. He offered to get a table while I changed from my swashbuckler's costume. Perhaps it was because I removed my rubber sword from my waistband and started stripping before I realized my error; or maybe it was the eye-patch, long hair and scraggly beard that caused the mass evacuation of maniacal, screaming women. Several accosted me. One bloodied my nose.

There I was, panicked with weapon in hand, partially naked and dripping with blood. Suddenly three male employees were dragging me out into the crowd. They were receiving accolades from everyone except my boss who snuck out the front door just before three police-men came through it with guns drawn.

As I was being cuffed, read my rights and shoved into a patrol car, I noticed my boss speeding from the parking lot. He had insisted on driving my car after the parade because he felt I deserved a rest. Now he was absconding with it!

Seeking a statement, reporters hounded the officers who shielded me from their access while several TV cameras recorded all of this.

Then I remembered my second reason for using the restroom: a response to the pressing needs of my bladder, now threatening to explode even in the absence of appropriate facilities.

Oh, why hadn't I heeded those adult diaper commercials?!!

As the uncontrollable secretion made its presence felt, a man in business attire opened the door and sat down beside me. Pulling an envelope from his valise, he said, "I have some papers here that need your signature, Mr. Edwards."

"Mr. Edwards!" he repeated, "Can you hear me? You appear lost in thought and you look unusually content for a man in your present circumstance."

"I was born under a water sign", I replied, "And I'm momentarily basking in its unanticipated influence. But who are you and how do you know my name?"

He said he was the producer of a TV show called "Why Didn't Someone Stop Me?"--- a successor to the old "Candid Camera" but with attitude. The papers would grant my consent to televise the incident. In exchange I would receive $5,000 to be divided equally with my boss who fully cooperated in the extensive staging that preceded it. We would also be their guests when it aired.

As I inked the document, he commented on the horrific odor in the car, to which I replied, "With all due respect sir, your antics have pissed me off!"

V

My Mother, The Shantytown Girl

When I was ten, I came across a picture of my mother, her two sisters and several other kids; many holding newspapers.

When I asked mom about it, all she said was, "Oh, that's from 1933 when I started *The Shantytown Girl's Club*. Someday, I'll tell you the whole story."

She died last year and, to my recollection, never kept that promise. It was long forgotten by us both until a lady from my photography club handed each of our members a copy of that very same photo two weeks ago. I knew I'd seen it before but didn't remember where until I viewed it again that evening.

Stunned, I phoned my Aunt Gertie, mom's youngest sister and the shortest person in the picture. Despite her eighty-four years, she knew exactly the photo in question.

"I always thought you knew about that, Chuckie," she said, "Come by tomorrow. I'll fill you in."

The next day, we met for lunch at her assisted-living facility in Sarasota. "Got a surprise for you, boy," she cackled reaching into her purse. "This the photograph you're speaking of?"

"My God Gertie, that's the picture I found when I was a kid, identical to the one my friend passed out yesterday; only it's a sepia Tintype."

"That's because it's the original. Your Grandpa Horace, took that snapshot himself with his converted Box Brownie."

"I didn't notice it when I was ten, Aunt Gertie, but there are a number of boys in..."

"Not a one!" she snapped, "Lots of us girls were afraid going into Hooversville. So we dressed like boys to feel safer?"

"No kidding?"

"You know, son, I'm wondering how your friend got hold of this. It's copyrighted. Maybe you should sue her; what's her name?"

"It's Jamima."

"Jamima, you say?"

"Yeah, it's her nickname. You see she makes the world's best pancakes"

"Ever check her recipes? Probably stole them too!"

"I'm sure she didn't, Gertie, but I'm here to learn about Shantytown Girls.

Following lunch, we sat on a veranda overlooking the Gulf of Mexico as she talked. "Your Granddaddy Horace was a wealthy man. He founded the Amalgamated Steelworks in St. Louis, not far from where that picture was taken. Sold the place for a fortune before he turned forty. He always drilled us kids on the need for public service in thanksgiving for the many blessings our family had received."

"I do remember that. He drilled me too."

"Probably because of this, your mother was already a zealot by the age of twelve. That's when she came up with that girl's club charity idea; right after hearing a sermon from our pastor one Sunday. He talked about the importance of newspapers to the Shantytown residents. Do you realize those papers were not only read by them but also used for blankets, towels, insulation, storage and even toilet tissue?"

"Really?"

"Yes, and other things too. Anyhow, you know your mother's Godfather was Zachary Robenns, right? Well, he was the publisher of the St. Louis Journal Crier. One day she asked him about the daily issues that went unsold. There were hundreds. After hearing about our Pastor's sermon, Zachary got hooked. He helped us and a few other girls set up monthly deliveries of surplus papers to Hooversville through a local moving company. When it ended three years later our contributions also included clothes, produce and day-old baked goods. I mean truckloads."

"That's it, Gertie?"

"Fraid so, boy. Everybody called us News Girls. And the only authorized copy of that picture still hangs today in a St. Louis Museum."

"My friend, Jamima, is really gonna be surprised."

"Yes, Chuck, especially when she hears from my lawyer!"

V I

A Good Deed, Indeed!

Kenny Fielding had served as an Army Combat Medic following three years of Pre-med studies at USI in Evansville. Upon his discharge, he intended to finish his education on Uncle Sam's nickel, planning to make as much money as possible before returning to school in September.

It was now mid-January in 1992; and, to date, his luck was running sour.

The recruiter had assured Kenny that Military-Health-Care training was in big civilian demand. But that recruiter wasn't familiar with Indiana's licensing regulations. He was lucky to have his job as an Orderly at St. Regis Hospital---though it paid little and offered no opportunity to utilize his considerable medical expertise.

Disappointment abounded. Nothing ever seemed to go his way!

Several weeks ago, when he struck up a conversation with a man seated across from him in the cafeteria, it seemed his fortunes were about to improve. "It's no accident I'm sitting here?" the man said, "I've had my eye on you for a while."

"Oh?"

"I'm Jeff Todd and I'm in medical sales. Do you mind answering a few questions?"

Becoming frustrated with the interrogation, Kenny asked, "Where is this going? I need to get back to work."

"I'm sorry, but there's a good reason. I thought you might be interested in a sales opportunity with my company."

"I'm not the sales type but thank you."

"No you're not---but you are our type. You have the poise and presence my firm looks for. We can teach you the rest."

Mr. Todd explained his territory was about to be vacated due to a promotion. The job offered a car and double Kenny's current income with substantial increases after training. Following several phone calls and some tweaking of his resume, an appointment was set with the corporate Human Resources manager for 11 AM that Thursday at the Hanncock Inn in Evansville.

Assuring Kenny the position was his to lose, Mr. Todd said, "When she flies back that afternoon, you'll be one of two finalists. My boss will be here the following week to make the final selection. He's my brother-in-law."

———

When Kenny left an hour early for that interview, he was sure Lady Luck was his co-pilot at long last. But soon, a rapid succession of break lights indicated a problem ahead. Hearing metal crushing, he turned and saw a car spinning across the road into several others. A man flew onto the highway with blood gushing from his thigh. Kenny sprang into action.

"Your tourniquet saved this man's life," a policeman said minutes after arriving. The Medi-copter crew echoed his sentiments. The dazed patient however felt otherwise yelling, "I'm losing my leg because of you, you sonofabitch? I hope I live long enough to sue your sorry ass for everything you're worth!"

Shocked by this response, Kenny got back into his car, thinking, *I just can't do anything right!*

Worse yet, it was now noon and there was no phone booth in sight. A message was waiting for him at the Hanncock Inn to call Mr. Todd who sadly advised there'd be no second chance to apply. The two candidates selected would have their final interview in the same hotel next Thursday morning, both well qualified for the position.

So stricken with grief and self-pity was Kenny that he skipped work that afternoon, going home instead. His anger mounting, he gathered up every religious artifact he owned. Stuffing them all into a bag, he headed to church, where he stood screaming maniacally, "Why do You hate me? What have I ever done to deserve Your wrath?"

"I curse this bag and everything in it!" he said, throwing it at the altar. "And you know that fairy tale about the Good Samaritan, well I curse that, too!"

———

On Monday, Kenny received a letter from the wife of the man whose life he'd saved, apologizing for her husband's behavior and requesting a 9:30 meeting Thursday morning at his rehab center a few blocks from the Hanncock Inn. "He understands now the enormous debt of gratitude our family owes you," it read.

A half-hour into that conciliatory meeting, a woman ran through the corridor screaming, "There's been a terrible accident!"

At 9:53 AM, an Air National Guard training flight had gone awry, crashing into the Hanncock Inn killing 16 people, including the applicants competing for Mr. Todd's vacancy and their interviewer. Kenny was stunned; he was supposed to have been one of those people.

The date was February 6, 1992.

When Kenny arrived home that night, a present was on his porch. Opening it, he broke into tears. It contained his Bible, crucifix, rosary and St. Christopher medal with a note, which read: I'm sorry My mysterious ways have caused you so much pain. I hope you forgive Me as I forgive you.

Yours eternally,
God

PART III
SHORT FABLES

VII

Staying the Path

Once upon a time very long ago, there lived a boy named Sam. His only goal in life was to someday live on the beach. Back then, before maps existed, finding the beach was difficult. Fortunately, he was friendly with an Oracle, who told him precisely which route to take.

When he had saved enough money for a small buggy, a donkey and a tent, Sam set about pursuing his dream. Surprisingly, the road was easily found and off he went.

The first day, the ride was pretty bumpy. The second day, he encountered potholes. On the third day, the potholes became craters. On the fourth day, when he was about to turn back in total frustration, he came upon a remarkably smooth road; so enticing, in fact, that the sun itself appeared to be caressing it at the horizon. And, lo and behold, it had a sign with an arrow on it, prominently displaying the word "Shortcut".

"My lucky Day," Sam shouted, "The remaining journey will be a pleasure".

For two magical days he enjoyed his good fortune until he realized he wasn't heading toward the beach at all; instead, he found himself back home.

"What happened?" he shouted at the Oracle, "I followed the exact road you told me to take."

"And how was the ride?" The Oracle responded.

"Terrible until I found the shortcut, then it was beautiful."

"That was your error," The Oracle chastised, "The road to the beach is filled with obstacles until it ends. And, when you took the shortcut, you only had one more bumpy hour to go before you reached the beach."

The moral of this story is: whenever you're working toward goals, resist shortcuts and learn to tolerate the bumps.

VIII

Zelda and Belinda

As tavern wenches go, Zelda was not one of the better lookers. From afar one could see she'd probably had her day; but up close, you knew it must have been generations ago. She was humble but very effective in her work, holding the respect of cohorts and patrons alike.

Zelda couldn't remember her childhood or when her auburn hair had turned to gray or even when her job had begun. It was as if she'd always been just this way. She worked at Mariner's Inn on a small English-populated island. Known as the Ancient Cay, it was not too far from Greece. The time was many, many centuries past...

——

As Fairy God-mothers go, Belinda was in a league all her own. She also lived on Ancient Cay, though nobody knew where. Pixie in stature, she wore a yellow-sequined tutu and an opal-studded tiara. Her locks were yellow as gold and, for those who'd actually seen Belinda; this was not only her most compelling feature, but also the source of her magic.

Though her legend was primarily known to the locals, many a visiting sailor attributed good fortune and calm seas to her personal intervention. Each benefactor, mired in crisis, received a strand of her hair and their problems turned into blessings.

———

Zelda, who lived in modest quarters behind Mariner's Inn, accepted the inexplicable fact that she and Belinda were actually one and the same person.

Though her life had not been particularly easy, Zelda knelt every night in prayer thanking God for the gifts and blessings He'd allowed her. Never once did she complain. Never once had she asked for more. It was during one of those sessions that the transformation first took place. Not questioning this, Zelda knew instinctively Belinda's mission was to assist those in dire need; but only people who counted their blessings in appreciation, nary anyone who dwelt in self-pity or cursed their misfortune.

———

And it came about, over time, that an Angel of the Lord God appeared one night to Zelda. No! She was Belinda! No, no, no...at that magical moment, there were now two; both Belinda and Zelda. She was one. She was both!

And the Angel, Morgahna, spake unto them, "You have served man-kind well and it is time for your reward. Forever hence, you shall be as one. And, at that moment, *Zelinda* was created, awaking in an enchanted cottage where her every need would be satisfied throughout eternity.

But, of course, Zelinda had started every morning like this since time began, hadn't she?

The moral of this story is: There is magic in counting your blessings; especially during troubled times.

IX

Ghost Writers in the Sky

I t seemed familiar to me; in fact, more than familiar, it was comfortable. But where was I and how did I get here? Checking out the premises, I determined it to be a cozy little house.

Could this be my home?

I didn't know but it appeared as though it were. The vistas outside assured me I was in a country club community. That made sense.

I couldn't tell if I were male or female; young or old. The contents of the closets and cabinets were of no help, though everything seemed to belong there.

My memory began to feed me scant glimpses of...of, oh yes, a bicycle going out beneath me; a doctor putting a mask over my face under that blinding light; the light intensifying ever so pleasantly...

Then there was that long tunnel. Did it take a microsecond or centuries to fathom ......

Venturing outside, I realized this wasn't a neighborhood at all.

I had just walked out through a door but when I looked back, there was no door in sight--nor any structure of any kind anywhere. Instead I was in a pastoral setting----the essence of tranquility---with nothing but lush greenery, babbling brooks and cascading waterfalls ensconced by the bluest of skies. And, oh that fragrance; how gently alluring it was.

This was manna for one's soul.

I wasn't alone. Countless indiscernible presences abounded. I couldn't see them, hear them, touch them or describe them. They were simply there; that's all I can say, emanating neither pain nor pleasure but only the simplistic joy of serenity.

One began to communicate with me in a nonlinguistic manner of concepts mutually exchanged and mutually understood. But to properly convey it, I must use words.

"New here, are you?" it asked.

"How can you tell?" I replied.

"The new ones always look around for that door."

Somehow I knew that names were non-existent here, each presence being distinct from every other but always recognizable and comprehended. "Where are we?" I asked.

"We are at the end and the beginning of a process that has taken us on a journey into and through a material existence; followed by one made up of only time and space," it answered, "Where we are now is where we started. It consists of nothing material and it is the total absence of time and space. Here, we merely have existence without definition."

"And, by the way," it continued, "All the sensory input you're feeling is nothing more than Heavenly fodder. It doesn't exist---just like the door you're seeking."

"Am I here eternally?" I asked.

"Yes, if by eternal, you mean: *always ending at the beginning*. And none of us know who we were in other dimensions; it's of no importance. We can only be sure we lived up to the requirements necessary to earn our present status."

"And what would that be"?

"We were all struggling but gifted writers who never gained prominence or much, if any, recognition. We all resisted the trappings of commercial gain, steadfastly clinging to the purity of individual artistic expression."

"I did that?"

"You must have or you wouldn't be here."

"I think I recall being ridiculed for liking adverbs, you know: words that end in 'LY'. Yes, yes and I remember the sheer agony of being criticized for too much verbiage...and...and putting commas in the wrong place. Am I being rewarded for suffering such excruciating humiliation?"

"You betcha!"

"But, what about the billions of people who never once put pen to paper?"

"Not for us to know, friend. Not for us to know. Same with the Homer's, Steinbeck's, Dostoevsky's and Twain's, who made a name for themselves. Their fate isn't ours to know either. But they ain't here, I'll tell you that!"

"Is there a purpose for us here?"

"Oh yes indeed! We've become muses to the fledgling authors of the universe. You're doing this already".

"I am? To all of them?"

"No, no, only to one! An ignorant, talentless soul; totally devoid of literary aptitude, named Charlie. About four months ago, in his world, you took over. He even joined a writing group, aptly called 'Writer's Bloc'. Poor fool; he's starting to believe he can write!"

"Why have I no recollection of working on his behalf?"

"Because in this dimension there is no past, present or future. But, it was his home you stepped from just before we met. Rest assured, you're doing a good job with him, even as we speak."

"...as we speak?"

"Yes. He's struggling with an assignment about a ghost who won't leave. His story is all coming from you---transformed into words, lines and paragraphs; plus a forbidden adverb or two."

"Oh, oh, now he's finished reading it to his group. Let's listen to their response.

X

Shoe Fly

In 1972, my wife and I heard these unthinkable words from our six-year-old daughter's physician: "Doreen has a rare form of incurable, infantile Leukemia."

Expected to live less than six months, God in His Divine Providence, gave our family an eighteen-month extension. What I remember most vividly about her remaining days was the sound of her flip-flops as she walked more and more slowly, eventually not walking at all. Her feet were in such excruciating pain but somehow those flip-flops made her mobility tolerable.

When she passed, we thought of encasing them in a shadow box or having them bronzed; maybe both. My mother-in-law insisted we do neither. "She loved those slip-ons, son. Even wore them to bed. Let them go with her. I'm sure that was what she expected."

So it was that little Doreen, wearing her Communion dress and her orange Flip-flops, was cremated on June 11th 1974. Her ashes were strewn off the shore of Lake Michigan where she spent her last days; this, with a full dispensation from our pastor who adored her.

Every year, her mother (now my ex-wife) and I meet with other family members in Grand Haven to commemorate this special child, whom we briefly had on loan from her Creator. My flight on route there each year is silently spent in solace, remembering the wonderful times we shared together. For the most part, people around me understood.

Not so, this year. Oh, she was pleasant enough, the elderly woman next to me. But, she would not shut up! Even, when I explained the solemn purpose of my trip.

"I get a little nervous in these things, my dear man," she said as we taxied toward our point of departure, "May I hold your hand until we're safely off the ground?"

How could I say no? Thirty minutes into the flight, however, she showed no signs of letting go. Then we hit a bump so severe the overhead popped open and a package of hers fell onto the floor next my seat. *Perfect timing,* I thought. Restoring it to the compartment above me would provide an opportunity to reclaim my arm.

It worked, though she continued her mindless chatter all the way to our arrival gate. I was concerned she'd solicit my assistance with her bags or maybe even ask for a ride. Being a man on a sacred mission, I needed to avoid this possibility. Not saying a word, I ducked into the restroom, staying there until the plane was almost empty. While I was pulling down my bag, the flight attendant called my attention to the package on the seat.

"Not mine," I explained," That belongs to the lady who sat next me."

"But, sir, that seat was unoccupied for the entire flight. Don't you remember, you were sleeping when that package fell in your lap and popped open. There are two orange slip-ons in there. You cried, saying they belonged to your daughter. I'll show you..."

But when she opened the box, the only thing inside was a coloring book called "This Little Piggy Went to Market". On the title page, these words were hand-printed in orange crayon: "All my love, Your little piggies", my pet name for Doreen's tortured feet.

PART IV
PLAY ON WORDS

XI

A Beatles' Dozen and Then Some

"Hey Jude," the dealer said when it was my turn to get cards, "How many?"

I was one of eight people who'd made it to the State Championship Poker finals—four at my table and four at another. Yesterday, there were twelve of us; by this time tomorrow, there would be only four. I stood a good chance of being one of them since the cards had been falling my way all afternoon. Elated because this hand was no different, I answered, "I want to hold."

"Your hand must be a good one Mr. Lucky," a familiar voice yelled from the bar. I was stunned when I realized it was my ex-wife and I owed her back alimony---almost two year's worth! The state capital was three hours from her home. Was this mere coincidence or had she followed me?

When I saw her standing there, I prayed God would let it be someone else who'd win this hand. Anyway, I've got a feeling the good Lord had never heard such a thing from a gambler and probably felt I misspoke. Thus, my full house took the pot---a big one, at that.

"Wait!" I shouted, "Can we take a break here? I'm down to my last cigarette."

In reality, all I really wanted was to confront my ex. Approaching her, I uttered, "Ah, the lovely Rita Maggie-Mae!"

"Maybe that's why I stopped getting your money last year, you lyin' piece of junk," she answered, "I'm now just Rita Maggie since I've deep-sixed your idiotic last name that everybody misspells. Soon I'll be re-married and it'll change for the better."

"Thank you girl, that's one excuse I hadn't thought of and you know what, the court might just buy into that. Judge Leonard ain't the quick-est horse out of the gate, dearie. I think we both agree there."

"You mean Judge Steven Leonard, do you?"

"Certainly, who else?"

"You mean Judge Steven David Leonard, Judee-pie?"

"I haven't got time for this nonsense, Rita, I need to use the john, buy some cigarettes and get back to the table before the cards get cold."

"You'll probably run into him then, he was headed that way a couple of..."

"Run into who?"

"Why, Mr. Slow-horse, himself: my fiancé Judge Leonard. He's been following your lucky streak for the past month and on the way here we stopped by the court-house."

"For what?"

"For a State Writ of Garnishment against all your winnings; twenty-thousand in back alimony and the rest for pain and misery!"

There's a sad ending to this story: in spite of all my efforts to the contrary, I still won a majority of the hands for the rest of the tournament, though Judge Slow-horse was good enough to let me keep carfare for my trip home.

NOTE: There are fifteen Beatles' song titles hidden in this story. How many can you find? Answers on page 102.

XII

Hunky Dory

My great grandparents, Zolton and Magda Nagy, came from Hungary. In their culture, the family Bible included the family history. When they died, it went to my maternal grandfather and he, in turn, bequeathed it to my mom. Recently, she willed it to me.

To my surprise, it contains a section called Kliséket, which means 'Cliché'. That's where I discovered that two popular American ones found their origin in the small village where my great grandparents were born. But according to my Uncle Steve, it was not only names that were changed by immigration officers at Ellis Island but also clichés.

The first Kliséket was a curse you would wish on your enemy. It has to do with Szalonna, which means bacon in my family's native tongue. While many cultures would put horseshoes over their door or harvest four-leaf clovers, Hungarians floated a chunk of bacon in their bathwater. This is a verifiable truth as any Gypsy will tell you.

So if you hated somebody and wanted to wish him bad luck, you would instruct him to *throw out his bacon with the bathwater,* which is the literal translation of the first cliché in our family bible: 'Dobja ki a fürdővízzel együtt a szalonna'.

The second had to do with our family business, Kidnapping, an honored profession in those days. Every morning, as Grandpa Zolton left for work, Magda gave him a tender kiss, saying "Hozza haza a baba!" which means 'Bring home the baby'.

Now, when they came through customs, the heartless attendants wanted nothing to do with foreign culture clichés so, before they would allow my ancestors entry into our country, the Klisékets had to be Americanized.

Thus the phrases 'Throw out the baby with the bathwater' and 'Bring home the bacon' were created.

XIII

Making A Dead Line

*D*edicated, with all due respect, to someone for whom the author has the highest regard

We had to make this dead line come back to life; somehow, some-way or so my boss was insisting.

"What line?" I queried.

"This ridiculous line of questioning you just sent me; you know, for tomorrow's Interrogatory."

"You mean the product liability case for the portable highchair with casters on it?"

"Exactly. The line you're suggesting I take on this is unmitigated rubbish. It's dead I tell you, dead. We need to make it pop. You've made it pop over, you imbecile!"

"Why do you refer to it as *dead*, though?"

"Well for one thing, it's drowning in adverbs and I'm afraid the President of my Creative Writing group has a mole in here. I just know she'll find out about it."

"And then what?"

"She has a way of knifing me with the skill of a literary surgeon. She even criticizes the way I wear my hat even though I love wearing it backwardly. Anyway, get those damnable A-words out of there. In fact, put a piece of tape over the letters *L* and *Y* on your keyboard just to be sure."

"But sir, I really don't think *Jointly* and *Severally* will have the same impact if you just say *Joint* and *Sever*."

Let's put it this way, if you can't find the means to make that dead line of questioning come alive in the next two hours, I will personally sever your joint. Got it, schmuck?"

"I'm positive you can't mean that, sir."

"Why is that?"

"Because *personally* is an adverb and that Grim Adverb Reaper lady is bound to find out!"

XIV

Chez Klee

(reverse these two words and what have you got?)

An Update on a Backward Community

Chez Klee is where I live and its goin to the dogs faster than a bat out of hell! For example, take my neighbor Jozef, for instance. He's always makin a mountain out of a molehill even when its as plain as the nose on your face that there ain't none. For instance, like the other day. I had bundled my trash like I always do before I sat it out believe me I done it really good. Neat as a pin and as snug as a bug in a rug it was.

Some how, some way it got ripped into. I think it was those greasy hooligans from the next block what done it. What is it about them people over there anyways? Do they own stock in plaster companys or what! I would rather have a thumbtack enema than traipse down that street of theirs. Great God in heaven, they got more statues on their lawns than Carters got liver pills. Or is it liver pools. I can't never figure that one out. But pools of liver sure ain't nice soundin'.

But as far as Jozef goes he's crazy. Comes poundin' on my door all bent out of shape with a handful of my trash ready to throw at me I guess. Well I was at the end of my rope with that fat slob. His old lady, Mimi, is even fatter. She has more chins than a Chinese phone book. I seen them chins once get in her way when she was tryin to tie her shoes on even. Think I'm lyin? Them two always smell so bad of garlic, I think if they was on the street when that trashman comes, they'll be picked up and tossed in the truck. Did you know their kind eats duck blood soup, too? Honest injun.

Ain't there somethin vampirish about garlic and blood? Hey maybe that's why his temper is always swarmin' like bees on honey. Or is that bears I don't know. Anyway, before he could get a word in edgewise I sprayed him with deodorant and slammed the door on him faster than Greeks lightin'.

Ever since he's been quiet as a church mouse since then.

More from backward Chez Klee to come and I'll write it much more better. You see, I ain't had both oars in the water for a coon's age. But. Hey does the Pope spit in the woods; or is it....hell, I don't know. Whatever...?

Yours Truly,

Trailer Jim-Bob Hoakie

XV

Making A Treasure Hunt

I was born in the mid-forties and my family was very poor. The oil stove in our small two-bedroom home was so ineffective the room I shared with my older brother stayed ice cold all winter.

When I was four, my father could finally afford a small heater for us and we put in between our beds. In addition to a stocking filled with candy and nuts, it was our only Christmas present that year.

My dad, who drove a Model A Ford, loved to hunt and fish; otherwise, most of our meals would have been meatless. He also was the only cab driver in a small village where some folks felt there was one taxi too many. So, it often sat idly in front of our house; never available for personal use.

We were the only family on our block who didn't own a pet. In truth, we couldn't afford to feed one.

"Momma's our pet!" Daddy often said, occasionally tossing her a biscuit---just to make his point, I guess. Then he would wink and mumble something about a bone, which I never fully understood. So, imagine the surprise when, on my fifth birthday, Dad announced my gift would be a dog.

He said his hunting trips might be more productive, if a dog went along. My mother was sure it would make her feel more secure. And, my brother felt his track practices could be more productive if a dog ran with him.

"What about me?" I said tearfully, "Isn't it my present?"

"You get to choose it!" my parents said in unison.

"You get to name it!" my brother added; and off we went to the pound!

Within minutes, I spotted the dog I wanted, which the attendant speculated was part Lab, part Collie and part United Nations. It didn't matter, she took to us all immediately and the feeling was mutual; though I thought I'd heard my mom whisper something to my dad about biscuits being okay to share; but the bone was off-limits.

Anyway, I named her "Treasure" because, to me, that's what she truly was!

Before that evening ended, we discovered she was completely housebroken. So housebroken, in fact, she even went outside to shed!

For my mother, Treasure indeed provided formidable security; especially when it came to bill collectors, for whom she possessed inbred disdain. My brother's track practices also improved with Treasure nipping at his heals whenever his pace slackened.

But for my father, Treasure was a monumental disappointment. "That damned dog simply will not hunt!" my father shouted after several futile hunting trips. Whenever he spotted a prey, Treasure barked until the animal fled. And, she immobilized dad with her attacks whenever he raised his rifle to shoot.

The principal at my brother's school was one of my father's regular passengers. They shared a passion for hunting. When Dad told him about Treasure's deficiencies in that regard, they decided there had to be a way to train her.

"Hey, why don't we have a contest to see if someone can make your dog hunt?" the principal said.

They soon agreed upon an appropriate prize: the first deer or pheasant shot with Treasure's help. In our depressed community, this could mean meat for an entire winter. Our local paper ran the story and the contest soon took place at my brother's school.

The room overflowed with eager contestants.

Attempting to quiet the crowd, the Principle grabbed a piece of chalk and wrote the word "TREASURE" on the board, announcing, "My friend's dog, Treasure, needs to be trained to hunt. The first one to do this wins our prize."

Many claimed they could do the job in three days; several asserting it required only two. A few felt one day was really all it would take. Then a scraggly little boy with ragged clothes said his family was starving and they really needed food.

"If I make Treasure hunt tonight, will you give my family the prize?"

"Of course we will!" the principal said, "But how ever do you intend to do this?"

Amid laughter and mockery, the feisty lad fought his way to the blackboard.

He erased the word "TREASURE" and wrote the word "HUNT" in its place. Faithful to his promise, he had made treasure hunt, everyone conceding he was the winner. His prize, however, would never materialize because Treasure remained unwavering in her commitment to protect other animals. But, because of the boy's original approach, a collection taken up among the other contestants yielded enough money to feed his family for the next year.

Like the author of this tale, that little boy often saw problems differently than everybody else.

PART V
SHORT & PERSONAL

XVI

My Roots

Memories of my childhood begin in an unfinished house my parents purchased for $4,400 in 1945. A skilled carpenter, my father meticulously turned it into a home using only hand tools given him by his immigrant grandfather. Because of the War, building materials were scarce, so he improvised. Once the inside was complete, his efforts were turned outdoors.

My dad sawed each piece of the white picket fence he erected in front of our home by hand. In similar fashion, he drilled every hole in the t-bar he used to construct the fence behind the house, completing it with chicken wire stretched with chains attached to the bumper of his car. A three-foot high accent fence bisected the back yard. My father made that with 4x4 posts through which copper tubing rails ran. He also built an arbor in the center, leading to a garden area. To the left were my mother's flowers and to the right we grew our vegetables. Roses and raspberry bushes would eventually cover both segments of the back yard fence and the arbor.

My impoverished parents created a warm, if not romantic, cottage environment totally out of place in a neighborhood I can charitably characterize as "Red-neck haven." Cars, with radios blaring, incessantly raced up and down our graveled street, often ending up in the ditch. Drinking, hooting, cussing and hollering were the norm throughout day and into the night. Gunfights were not uncommon. A fat smelly man at the end of our block got his liquor and other favors from the locals by allowing them to have their way with his underage daughters, a foot or two into the woods.

Racial prejudice ran rampant against the black folks who lived only a block away. Our neighborhood was separated from theirs by George Early Road, a demarcation line more steadfast than the Berlin Wall would be a decade or so later. And anybody who even thought about selling their home to a "G-D N-word" was assured of having it burned to the ground most likely with the family still in it!

Though this rowdy faction set the neighborhood tone, there was also a more mainstream element; and, somehow my family and I found and bonded with these good folks. Neither of my parents ever finished high school but they were God-fearing people with high ideals, insisting my sister and I march to a similar drummer.

As I look back now, I realize their genius in never attempting to shield us kids from life as we found it. Whether or not that was a conscious decision, it was certainly the correct one. Life is not fair. Some people are bad. Blatant avoidance weakens. Skillful avoidance strengthens. Blatant confrontation can be more cowardly than courageous confrontation chosen as a last resort.

In my neighborhood, I was taught to skillfully navigate life by being tossed into its treacherous waters. No life jackets. No bumper cushions. No training wheels. I thank God for His infinite wisdom in starting my life out in this way.

XVII

Lessons From Down Under

In the summer of 1963, my mind was in the gutter, literally. I was employed by the City of Dodge Park's Sewer Department. Deciding to accept that position over an offer to work on a Detroit River excursion boat was a gargantuan step toward adulthood.

Friends and family thought I'd gone mad turning down that dream job, but I hadn't. I simply grew up. You see, there was more money to be made in fewer hours going the Ed Norton route. Plus, my shift was 7AM to 3:30, freeing evenings and weekends to work elsewhere.

Footing my own expenses, every cent was needed to complete my junior and senior years at Eastern Michigan University including room and board. My '57 Chevy wasn't up to a 60 mile commute daily nor was my constitution.

Learning a critical lesson even before starting that abominable job, I discovered what it meant to be a man setting a life-long decision-making pattern in the process. Seldom if ever have I chosen the easier path since then, unless it appeared to be the correct one.

I remember Councilman Sammy Samson graphically describing the maudlin perils of working underground in 90 degree-plus weather. I'd be knee-deep in human excrement with a shovel, a bucket and an extra-wide brimmed hat eight hours a day. Telling me no college kid ever lasted beyond the first week, he cautioned, "Remember, that excursion-boat job won't be waiting for you, son, if you do decide to quit. Then what will you do?"

In spite of his warnings and numerous attempts by the regulars to sabotage my three-month tenure, I survived because I had to, gaining the respect of all by summer's end.

There was another lesson I learned working there, equally important to my future as a businessman. It occurred a few weeks after everyone realized there was nothing they could subject me to, underground, that would cause me to leave. So, I was "promoted" to the illustrious position of jackhammer operator. And that came close to doing me in. The morning I started, I was shown only how to turn it on and off before being escorted to the job site.

"You just break it up, college-boy," I was ordered, "We'll do the hard part and lug it over to the truck."

That hammer must have weighed fifty pounds and, within minutes, it seemed my eternal rest was imminent! How I lasted eight hours, remains an enigma. Even more surprising, I somehow showed up the next day; though unsure of whether I was there to work or to resign.

Greeted by laughter and a round of applause, I was stunned.

"Ain't none of us could've lasted the day doin' what you did yesterday, professor," the foreman said, "You really showed us somethin' comin' back this morning."

"I see people working these all the time," I replied. "What do you mean *you guys can't*?"

"Why, you just described your problem, son. What you really seen was the jackhammer workin' while the operator holds it. That's all you have to do: just hold it. It does the rest all by itself. You were jerkin' that som'bitch around like it was a pick or somethin'. That's why it got the best of you. You college kids ain't got no horse sense whatsoever!"

Thereafter, it became a piece of cake, cliché notwithstanding.

Every boss needs to learn the critical lesson I gleaned from that event. Translated it means this: employees perform best when you stay off their back and don't jerk them around. Trusting them to do their work makes a manager's job much easier.

XVIII

I Give Up!

A Politically Incorrect Essay

The spirit of the current Holiday Season, in my opinion, has been indelibly corrupted by the absurd positions of the "politically correct" Radical Left and the equally polarizing supersensitivy of the Radical Right.

I am shocked that many of my friends and neighbors have blindly allowed themselves to become active pawns in this trivial battle of labeling one another by the words used in expressing honest and cheerful sentiments of (what used to be called) the *season that brings us all together*.

For decades I was used to hearing and saying such phrases as: *What are you doing for the Holidays* (which, if one looks closely, is clearly a derivative of "Holy Days"), *Sing in the Holidays, Home for the Holidays, Holiday shopping, It's the Holiday season* etc., etc---Hey!! I am even guilty of staying at the *Holiday Inn*, but now I suspect Bing Crosby, himself, would shun that movie, which ushered in this endearing term, for fear of offending someone.

Where I come from, the Holiday Season (an appropriate characterization, to my way of thinking) begins on Thanksgiving and continues well into January to account for a variety of Orthodox traditions, and encompasses a plethora of diverse ethnic beliefs and rituals. So, for 70 years (OK, the first year I could only say something like "gaga-pooh"), without giving much thought to it, I have sincerely wished my friends and neighbors my heartfelt expression of peace and goodwill: "Happy Holidays!"

Around fifteen years ago I sadly found myself in the uncomfortable position of justifying this lifelong tradition because more and more people want to classify it as a political statement, which simply poisons the true sentiments for which it is meant.

So, I want to go on record to my radical left friends and my radical right friends:

There are lots of Holidays (holy or otherwise) is this wonderful season and I truly hope each and every one is happy, merry and blessed for you and yours. If you still choose to lecture me for my sincere expression of good will, well, here is a non-political term with universal meaning for all: BAH HUMBUG!!!

The personal faith of my youth, which remains the foundation of my core values, is all about *love* and *tolerance*. Its tenets are based on *good will* and *peace on earth* and *treating your neighbor with the same consideration you expect* in return. It is not divisive but inclusive; it is not about self-righteousness but about humility; it does not seek retribution but turns the other cheek; it does not judge unless one expects similar scrutiny and, most importantly, it teaches, among other things, that by your "acts" you will be known.

So, to the majority of my friends and neighbors, who are politically in the middle, as am I, and, thus, wishing to be comfortably insulated from this nonsense, I thank you for taking my words at face value and for accepting me as I am.

In my opinion, it is the most God-like "act" we can perform for one another.

PART VI
SILLY POEMS

XIX

My Flawed Existence---A True Confession

I've overcome drinking,

and smoking as well.

I go to the gym,

and work-out like hell!

My closets aren't cluttered,

and I keep my place neat.

But I've never figured out,

how to fold a fitted-sheet!

X X

Elevated Love

The couple was bickering,
Who knows what about.
The lights began flickering
and then they went out.

United by this crisis,
they were stuck between floors,
no apparent devices,
to pry open the doors.

"Fear not my loved one,
we're gonna make it through."
"I realize that hon-bun,
but what shall we do?"

"Here's something we spoke of
many times before:
'Tis better to make love
Than it is to make war."

The lights began flashing,
and then they went POP.

The couple lie thrashing.
It was too late to stop.

The doors would soon open,
exposing their lust.
But they were still gropin'
No time to adjust.

I'm delighted to say
They completed their bout,
'cause nine months to the day,
yours truly popped out!

XXI

Holy Rodentia!

There once was a church mouse named Fred,

Who feasted on unleavened bread.

That would've been fine,

But he doused it with wine,

That went straight to his little old head.

As I sang from my choir loft perch,

I saw penitents suddenly lurch.

Then we heard from the preacher,

About that wee drunken creature,

Who was wreaking such havoc in Church.

XXII

A Hurricane Carol

With apologies to Clement Moore

T'was the night of the hurricane,
and all through that horrible bout,
nothing in my home was working,
because my power had just gone out.

The plywood was hung,
on my windows with care,
anticipating the fury,
that soon would be there.

My neighbors in a dither,
and I in a fit,
were all scared to death
our homes would be hit.

My children were nestled
up north in their beds,
My last Will and Testament
Dancing in their heads.

Mr. Charles F. Pletcher

When out on the lawn,
there arose such a clatter,
I sprang from my closet
to see what was the matter.

Away to the window,
like an eagle I flew,
smashing my head on the plywood,
that was blocking my view.

I then tried the door,
which I could open but a crack.
I was blown to the floor,
landing flat on my back.

But for a brief instant,
there was a sight to be seen,
and I knew in a flash,
it had to be Jeanne.

With plundering power,
her forces they came,
and whistled and shouted,
their destructive refrain.

To the top of my porch
to the bottom of my wall,
she blew away and blew away.
Never once did she stall!

Now, frightened and trembling,
in my closet with grief,
I munched on cold cereal,
and a can of corned beef.

A night to remember,
no lights, phone or cell,
Del Webb may be Paradise,
but this felt like Hell.

Creeping back to the door
for another quick glance,
I was slapped in the face,
by someone's soaked underpants.

'Tis the day after the Hurricane,
and all over my block,
brave neighbors step out,
and begin taking stock.

To a rap on my door,
I answered, "Who's there?"
T'was only my neighbor,
In search of her lost underwear.

Written in loving memory of Jeanne; may she rest in peace!!

XXIII

Ode To An Aging Crittaphobiac

'Twas the night before her birthday,

and, all over her house,

she was shaking a broom,

in fear of a mouse.

The doors were all sealed,

with exceptional care.

But she still cried to heaven,

"Let no gecko enter there!"

When under her bed,

she heard something shake,

she begged once again,

"May it not be a snake!"

Now down on her knees,

she prayed with the jitters,

"For my birthday, dear God,

Don't send me no critters!"

XXIV

The Steady Weathercock

There once lived a weathercock named Eddy

who could not bend nor sway.

His parents who were both unsteady

were ashamed he turned out that way.

"Never holding a position is what weathercocks do,"

they preached to him in vain.

"If every weathercock acted like you,

why, directions would all be inane!"

Try as he might poor Eddy remained

as rigid as rigid could be.

His family had now been indelibly stained,

Oh, how ashamed was he.

"Are you familiar with the word mutation?"

an oracle asked him one day,

"For, in my humble estimation,

it's the reason you're unable to sway.

You're a step ahead of the rest of your breed,

the beginning of defiant traditions.

Your heritage will be revered, indeed.

But your family's will spawn politicians.

Mr. Charles F. Pletcher

BEATLES SONG TITLES IN ORDER OF APPEARANCE

1) Hey Jude
2) Yesterday
3) Because
4) I Want to Hold Your Hand
5) When I Saw Her Standing There
6) Let It Be
7) I've Got a Feeling
8) Wait
9) I'm Down
10) Lovely Rita
11) Maggie Mae
12) Money
13) Junk
14) Thank You Girl
15) Misery

www.ingramcontent.com/pod-product-compliance
Lightning Source LLC
Chambersburg PA
CBHW020617130626
46552CB00003B/1017